TEEN TITANS

Cyborg, Come Home!

Adapted by Tracey West
Based on the episode *Divide and Conquer* written by David Slack
Illustrated by Kevin MacKenzie

Scholastic Inc.

New York   Toronto   London   Auckland   Sydney
Mexico City   New Delhi   Hong Kong   Buenos Aires

ISBN: 0-439-63620-5

TEEN TITANS and all related characters and elements are trademarks of DC Comics © 2004. All rights reserved.

Published by Scholastic Inc.
SCHOLASTIC and associated logos are trademarks and/or registered trademarks of Scholastic Inc.

12   11   10   9   8   7   6   5   4   3   2   1   4   5   6   7   8/0

Designed by Carisa Swenson
Printed in the U.S.A.
First printing, August 2004

Chapter One

Teen Titans, Go!

Sirens wailed across the prison yard. The prison guards sprang into action. What their security screens showed couldn't be true, could it?

Nobody was breaking out of prison. Someone was breaking *in*.

Well, not some*one*, exactly. More like some-*thing*. A huge creature that looked like it was made of concrete was smashing through the prison walls. It had legs like tree trunks, massive arms, and a square head. Red eyes glowed in its concrete face.

The guards ran up behind the creature and lift-ed their weapons.

"Fire!" someone shouted.

The creature turned, its red eyes blazing. Blue laser blasts shot out of the weapons, but they didn't harm the creature at all.

"Aaaargh!" With a mighty cry, the creature stomped one of its huge legs on the ground. Chunks of pavement broke off, flying at the guards. The creature grunted and continued inside the prison.

Then a voice rang out through the night.

"You know, Cinderblock, normally the bad guys break *out* of jail!"

The cry came from a small boy with green hair. He swooped into the room with another boy who was wearing a black mask, a red shirt, green tights, and a yellow cape.

"I can think of five good reasons why you don't want to break in," the masked boy said.

Cinderblock groaned. That could only mean one thing.

The Teen Titans had arrived.

Robin, the boy in the mask, jumped in front of

Cinderblock. "One!" he cried.

A girl with long red hair flew next to him. "Two!" yelled Starfire.

Green-haired Beast Boy sprang next to Starfire. "Three!"

Raven, a girl in a hooded blue cape, swooped in next. "Four!"

And, finally, came half-human, half-robot Cyborg, whose bulging arms and legs were almost as massive as Cinderblock's. "Five!" he boomed.

Robin grinned. "No matter how you do the math, it all adds up to you going down," he said. "So, are you going to go quietly?"

"Or is this going to get loud?" Cyborg asked.

Cinderblock didn't want anyone to get in his way, *especially* the Teen Titans.

"*Aaaargh!*" he cried angrily. He charged at the teen super heroes.

"Titans, go!" Robin cried.

Robin began the attack. He jumped up, spinning in midair. Then he sent his disk-shaped weapon hurling at Cinderblock. The metal weapon struck Cinderblock's hard head and bounced off.

Then Starfire flew at Cinderblock. Being from another planet gave Starfire some cool powers — like the ability to shoot green laser beams from her eyes. Starfire zapped Cinderblock with a green blast, sending him reeling.

Cyborg attacked next, whamming Cinderblock with a huge punch. Cinderblock punched back,

and their big fists locked. Cyborg and Cinderblock both went tumbling backward.

Beast Boy transformed into a green bird. He flew around Cinderblock's face, trying to confuse him further. Cinderblock brushed away Beast Boy and stomped across the floor, trying to get away.

But Raven flew in front of him, blocking his way. She raised her arms in the air.

"Azarath, Metrion, Zinthos!" she chanted.

The concrete floor in front of her broke into huge pieces. They formed a wall between her and Cinderblock. He turned around angrily.

Robin and Cyborg ran at Cinderblock. But the huge villain sent them both packing.

Starfire zoomed in next. She held out her palms, and a green fireball appeared in each one. She hurled the fireballs at Cinderblock, but they missed. Before Starfire could fly away, Cinderblock grabbed her.

Chapter Two

Sonic Bust

Starfire smiled sweetly at Cinderblock. "I am sorry to disappoint you," she said. "But I am stronger than I look."

Starfire's eyes glowed green as she powered up for the attack. Then she aimed a powerful kick at Cinderblock's chest. The kick sent the big villain flying backward.

As Cinderblock climbed back to his feet, Beast Boy transformed from a bird into a fierce, green Tyrannosaurus rex. The T rex charged at Cinderblock, but the concrete monster was ready. He slammed his huge fist into the T rex, sending the dinosaur flying through the air.

Across the room, Raven was readying for

another attack.

"Azarath, Metrion, Zin —" She stopped in mid-sentence. The huge T rex was speeding right toward her. . . .

Luckily, Beast Boy transformed back into his original form just in time. He crashed into Raven, sending them both sprawling.

Raven got to her feet and smoothed out her cape.

"Uh, watch out for falling dinosaurs?" Beast Boy joked.

Raven scowled.

"I'm going to leave you alone now," Beast Boy said, darting away.

In the meantime, Robin had jumped onto Cinderblock's back, wrapping his arms around the creature's thick neck. Cinderblock roared and waved his arms, trying to shake Robin loose.

"Thrashing only makes me hold tighter!" Robin quipped.

Cinderblock stumbled against a gate of metal bars. He latched onto a wide steel beam, then pulled it loose from the wall. With a grunt, he slammed the beam over his right shoulder.

Robin jumped off Cinderblock's back to avoid the blow. He landed next to Cyborg.

Cyborg grinned. "Now there's an idea," he said.

Cyborg might not have been as massive as Cinderblock, but he was nearly as strong. He ripped off a steel beam for himself and charged at Cinderblock.

BOOM! BOOM! The sound of metal against metal echoed throughout the prison as Cyborg

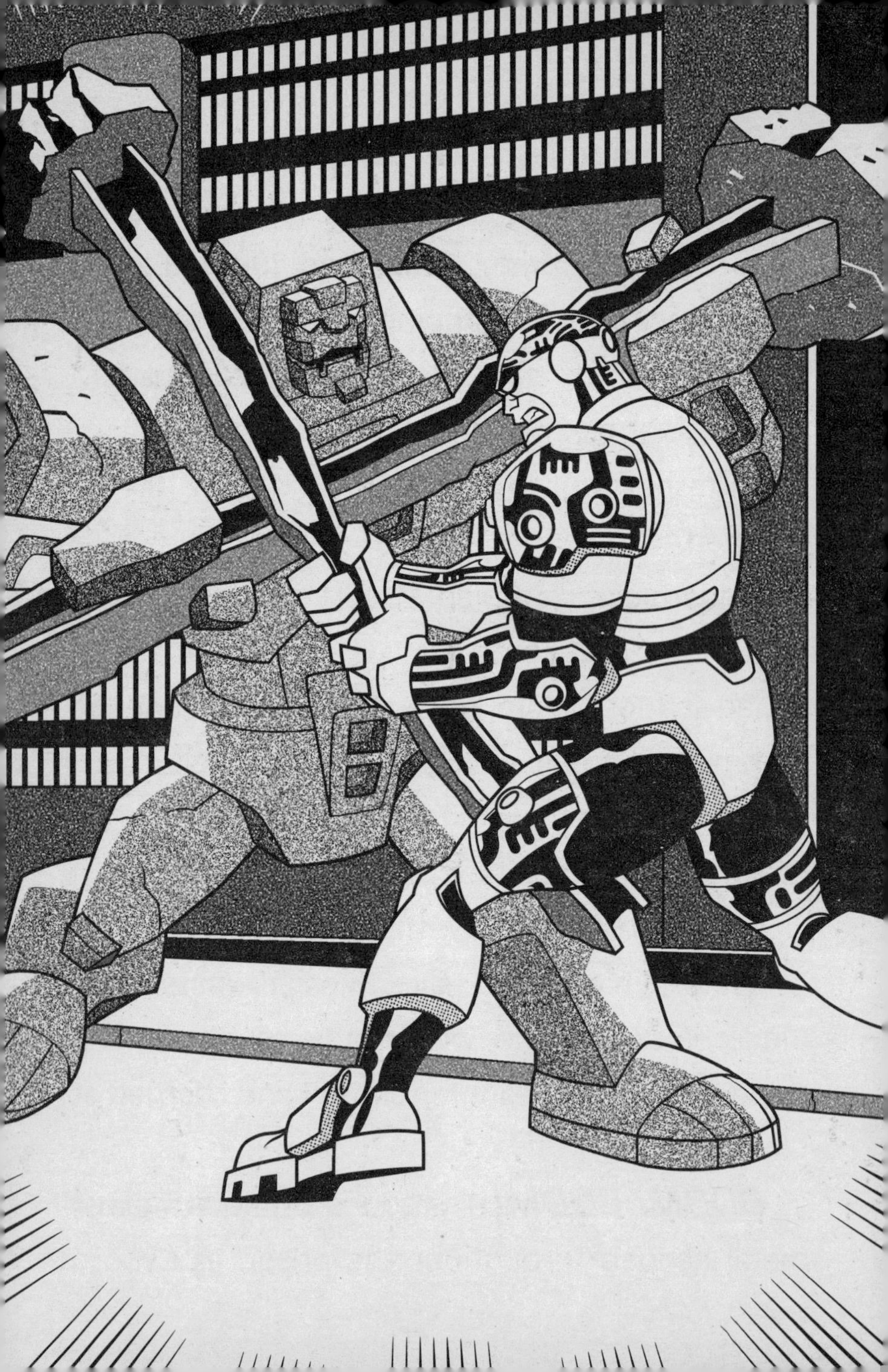

and Cinderblock exchanged blows.

Cinderblock roared with anger as Cyborg matched him, blow for blow. Then Cinderblock changed tactics. He held the steal beam like a baseball bat and slammed it into Cyborg's metal chest.

Slam! Cyborg fell on his back. Cinderblock moved in to deliver one last blow.

But Starfire flew in front of Cinderblock. She hurled a ball of green energy at the steel beam in his hand. The beam drooped, like a piece of limp spaghetti. Starfire's blast had transformed the metal.

"Aaargh!" Cinderblock roared.

Robin could see that Cinderblock was growing frustrated. The team was wearing him down. It would just take one big move to finish him off. And he knew just the move. Robin turned to Cyborg.

"Wanna give this guy the Sonic Boom?"

Cyborg raised his right arm. His metal hand

retreated inside his arm, and a barrel-shaped weapon took its place.

"I've got the sonic if you've got the boom!" Cyborg replied.

The Sonic Boom never failed. Robin and Cyborg practiced it all the time. They built up momentum by spinning through the air. Then they combined their most powerful weapons in one huge blast: Robin's exploding disk, and Cyborg's laser blast.

Cinderblock had already started to run down a narrow corridor in the prison.

"Yo, blockhead!" Robin cried out.

Robin and Cyborg chased after Cinderblock. They each ran up one side of the wall and flipped over, landing on the floor. Then they each flipped again, going faster. Then they flipped for the third time, and their feet got tangled together! Robin and Cyborg slammed into the floor, then went sliding in different directions. Cyborg's laser weapon fired, blasting Starfire and Beast Boy. Robin's disk slid out of his hand and exploded in a

blaze of white light — right in front of Raven. When the smoke cleared, the Teen Titans were all okay. But Cinderblock was nowhere in sight. He had slammed his way through the prison, breaking open jail cells as he moved. Now the hallways were crowded with prisoners trying to escape.

Robin grimaced. "Whoops!"

Chapter Three

Prisoner 385901

The prisoners scrambled around, looking for a way out. Robin hesitated. He hated to see Cinderblock get away. But the Titans had to take care of the prisoners — now.

"Let's get 'em!" Robin yelled.

The Teen Titans sprang into action, rounding up the prisoners.

That left Cinderblock to complete his mission. He slammed his way through wall after wall until he reached a door deep in the heart of the prison. The sign on the door read:

Cinderblock ignored the sign. He pushed down the heavy metal door.

PRISONER 385901 ABSOLUTE SILENCE!

The room was dark. Screens lined the curved walls of the room. Images of blue liquid washed across the screens, and soft, peaceful music floated through the room.

None of this interested Cinderblock. He had come for one thing only: Prisoner 385901.

A glass tank hung down from the ceiling, a few feet above the floor. Blue liquid filled the tank. And floating, suspended in the liquid, was the prisoner. A thin man with brown hair, he looked completely harmless. And he was fast asleep.

But Cinderblock knew better. With a grunt, he pulled down the tank from the ceiling, tearing it away from the metal cables that held it. He hoisted the tank over his shoulder. Inside, the prisoner still slept.

Cinderblock stomped his foot. A huge hole appeared in the floor. Cinderblock vanished through the hole.

He had the prisoner. The Teen Titans had failed to stop him.

His boss would be pleased.

Chapter Four

I Quit!

The Titans had rounded up most of the prisoners. But a few had spotted the open gates. They made a run for them.

"I think we're going to make it!" one cried.

Then, before their eyes, the gates flew through the air and reattached, slamming shut in front of them. Raven floated down, blocking their way.

"Think again," she said gravely.

The Teen Titans stood outside the prison and watched as the guards led the remaining prisoners safely inside.

"Jailbreak? I don't see any jailbreak," Beast Boy said with satisfaction.

But Robin was still steamed about losing

Cinderblock.

"None of us would have seen a jailbreak if Cyborg hadn't messed up," he snapped.

Cyborg looked down at his friend. "Me? I messed up nothing. *You* got in my way."

Robin didn't back down. "You were too far forward, and Cinderblock got away because of it."

"You're saying this is *my* fault?" Cyborg looked stunned.

"Want me to say it again?" Robin asked.

Starfire stepped between them. "Stop!" she cried. "No more mean talking."

Robin turned his back on Cyborg, and Cyborg did the same to him.

Beast Boy tried to ease the tension. "Yeah, if you two are going to fight, we need time to sell tickets."

But Cyborg and Robin weren't laughing.

Raven sighed. "Cinderblock escaped," she said. "No amount of yelling will change that. So stop acting like idiots and let's go home."

Robin and Cyborg walked away from each

other in opposite directions.

"Loser," Robin muttered under his breath.

"Jerk," Cyborg said.

The two turned around. "What did you say?!" they asked at the same time.

The two friends were in each other's faces now.

"You have a problem, tin man?" Robin asked.

"Yeah," Cyborg replied. "It's four feet tall and smells like cheap hair gel."

Starfire, Raven, and Beast Boy watched help-lessly as the two hurled insults at each other.

"Well, you're an oversized clutch and you smell like motor oil!" Robin fumed.

"You're bossy, you're rude, and you've got no taste in music!" Cyborg shot back.

Robin's face flushed with anger. "I don't even know why you're on this team!"

"That makes two of us!" Cyborg bellowed. "I quit!" The rest of the Titans watched, stunned, as Cyborg stomped away.

Chapter Five

Plasmus

The remaining Teen Titans headed back to headquarters in a daze. Meanwhile, in a secret hideout across the city, a man sat on a tall chair. Machines buzzed and whirred all around him. The man, Slade, sat in the shadows, waiting.

Then the sound of heavy footsteps echoed through the hideout. Cinderblock stomped up in front of Slade and slammed the tank, still holding the sleeping prisoner, on the floor.

Slade leaned forward, pleased. "Cinderblock, I see your mission was a success," he said. "Good. We will proceed with phase two. Wake him."

Cinderblock grunted as he twisted open the

round lid on top of the tank. Steam escaped as the blue liquid inside the tank evaporated.

The floating man opened his eyes. A look of shock crossed his face.

"I'm awake?" he asked, unbelieving. "I can *never* be awake. I'm only human while I'm sleeping!"

Slade smiled a snakelike smile. "But for what I have in mind, your human form is useless. I need Plasmus."

Slade sat back and watched. It didn't take long. The man in the tank began to transform. His human form seemed to melt, turning into a mass of gooey flesh.

The monster grew larger and larger, breaking through the sides of the tank. Shattered glass flew everywhere, and white smoke filled the air.

Plasmus had arrived.

The creature was twice as wide and twice as tall as Cinderblock. Its red, bloblike body moved in waves with each grunt the monster made. Its head was a shapeless form with two big eyes and a gaping mouth.

"Finally," said Slade, "I have what I need to accomplish my goal. The Teen Titans will fall!"

Chapter Six

The Pudding of Sadness

Robin, Starfire, Raven, and Beast Boy slouched back to Teen Titan's headquarters. Normally, the building — a tall, *T*-shaped structure overlooking the river — was filled with noise. Noise like Beast Boy listening to CDs, or Robin and Cyborg joking around. But today, the tall tower was quiet.

Losing Cinderblock was bad enough, but losing Cyborg — well, that was terrible.

Robin wandered off while Raven, Beast Boy, and Starfire settled in the main room. The Titans spent most of their time in this room, which held just about everything they needed — supercomputers for crime-fighting, a refrigerator full of (mostly) mold-free food, a giant TV screen, and a complete communications center.

Beast Boy picked up the phone and dialed Cyborg's number. All he got was a message: "This is Cyborg. I'm either in the gym, playing game station, or kicking bad-guy butt. Leave a message."

Beast Boy frowned. "Hello, Cy! Pick up! Pick up!" he said, pacing across the floor. "I know you're there. The phone is built into your arm."

But Cyborg didn't pick up. Sighing, Beast Boy hung up the phone.

Starfire floated over to Beast Boy, holding a bowl and a spoon. She dipped the spoon into the bowl and shoved a lump of gray mush into Beast Boy's mouth.

"Taste!" she said enthusiastically.

Beast Boy's eyes became as wide as saucers. He fell to the floor, clutching his throat. He spit out the mush, then wiped his tongue with his hands.

"What is that? Cream of toenails?"

Starfire shook her head. "The Pudding of Sadness," she explained. "It's what the people of my planet eat when bad things happen."

Starfire ate a spoonful of the pudding. She grimaced, swallowed, and made a horrible face. Then Starfire smiled. She had made the pudding perfectly!

She floated over to Raven, who was entering data on one of the computer screens on the wall.

"Try," Starfire said, holding out the bowl. "The displeasing taste will ease your mind."

"My mind is never troubled," Raven said in her usual calm voice. "People come. People go. It's pointless to be upset about Cyborg."

But as soon as Raven said Cyborg's name, her purple hair stood on end. The computer screen

shattered behind her.

Starfire raised an eyebrow. Raven might be acting like nothing was wrong, but her telekinetic powers showed the truth.

"What?" Raven asked.

Starfire floated over to Robin next. He was standing in front of one of the large windows in the tower, looking out over the river.

"Here, Robin," Starfire said, lifting up a spoonful

of pudding. "You must need this most of all, since, well . . ." Her voice trailed off. Starfire didn't want to say it, but Robin *had* started the fight with Cyborg. She knew he must be feeling guilty.

But Robin didn't show it. "I'm fine," he said. Then he walked away. "Who knows?" he muttered. "Maybe we're better off without him."

Robin went to the Teen Titans' gym and headed straight for the punching bag.

"Ya! Ya! Ya!" he cried. He delivered punch after punch. Then he pounded the bag with kung fu–style kicks. It felt good to let off steam.

Then, out of the corner of his eye, Robin saw the weight bench. The bars were stacked with heavy weights — just as Cyborg had left them.

Robin sighed. He just wanted to forget about Cyborg. He left the gym and headed for the kitchen.

He found Beast Boy struggling with a heavy stack of dirty dishes.

"Yo!" Beast Boy called out. "Whose turn to do dishes?"

Robin sighed again. "Cyborg," he said. Without saying a word, he took a dish from the top of the pile and began washing it.

Robin finished all the dishes, but he still felt restless. Maybe a video game would take his mind off things. He hooked up the game station and started to play, blasting boulders in midair with a laser cannon. Before long, he forgot all about Cyborg.

"All right!" Robin shouted when he finished. "New high score!"

The screen flashed. Cyborg's name appeared, with his score underneath. Then Robin's name appeared above it, with Robin's new high score. Robin's name smashed down on Cyborg's name and replaced it.

For the first time, the impact of the fight with Cyborg hit him. Robin had been wrong, he knew it. The messed-up move was just an accident. Robin had felt bad about letting Cinderblock get away, and he took it out on Cyborg. Now Cyborg was gone, and there was no way to tell him he was sorry.

Robin headed down a corridor to Cyborg's room. He pressed a button, and the metal door slid to the side. Cyborg's room was neat, as always. And dark. It was clear that no one had been there for a while. Robin walked over to a bookshelf and picked up a picture of him and Cyborg, smiling and goofing around.

"I'm sorry," Robin said softly.

Suddenly, an alarm rang. Robin rushed to the main

room and found Raven, Starfire, and Beast Boy staring at a computer screen. It showed a blueprint of the city with a flashing white dot on a factory downtown.

"Cinderblock strikes again?" Robin asked.

"You wish," Beast Boy said. "Whatever that thing is, it's a lot bigger than Cinderblock."

"We can take care of it," Robin said. To himself, he added, *with or without Cyborg.*

Robin took a deep breath. "Come on, Titans," he cried. "Let's go!"

Chapter Seven

Let Him Have It!

The Teen Titans raced downtown. They flew inside the factory. A huge machine took up most of the space. A metal chute on top of the machine poured green goo into barrels as they rolled along on a conveyor belt. The goo looked and smelled like some kind of chemical waste.

Plasmus waited for the barrels at the other end of the moving belt. He picked them up, one by one, and gulped down the green chemicals inside.

Robin couldn't believe his eyes. What kind of creature was this? Plasmus had grown larger. Now he was a *huge* red blob. His head nearly reached the tall ceiling of the warehouse. And what was he doing eating that goo?

"That stuff can't be good for you," Robin quipped.

Plasmus threw an empty barrel aside and let out a large burp.

"Nice one!" Beast Boy said, impressed.

Plasmus curled his blobby hands into fists. He grunted, and streams of red ooze shot out of his chest — straight at Robin! Robin expertly dodged the red blobs and jumped up onto a wooden crate, out of the way.

"Star!" he called out. "Let him have it!"

Starfire flew straight at Plasmus. An electric green glow shone from her eyes. She extended her hands, shooting out a giant ball of energy.

Wham! The balls exploded through Plasmus's chest, leaving a gaping hole as wide as a manhole cover.

Starfire looked worried. "Did I let him have it too much?"

But Plasmus recovered quickly. Red blobby flesh flowed in, filling up the hole.

"I'm thinking not enough!" Beast Boy said.

Plasmus extended his left arm. It stretched and stretched at superspeed until it almost grabbed Starfire. Raven came to the rescue, flying into Starfire and knocking her out of harm's way.

Robin frowned. Starfire's blasts could take down almost anything.

"Maybe he just needs to chill," Robin said. He threw his disk at Plasmus's extended arm. This time, instead of exploding, the disk blasted Plasmus with subzero ice. The arm froze from the fingers all the way up to the creature's shoulder.

"*Aaaargh!*" Plasmus gave an angry roar. He smashed the icy arm against the wall. The arm broke right off! Right away, another blobby arm formed, replacing it.

Starfire flew at Plasmus again, shooting blast after blast. Beast Boy transformed into a pterodactyl and flew alongside her. While Plasmus tried to dodge the blasts, Beast Boy lunged at Plasmus with his sharp claws.

Plasmus countered by shooting a small river of red goo at the two of them. The sticky mess caught them both in midair just as Starfire was about to shoot another energy ball. The ball exploded in front of them, sending them both tumbling to the ground.

The Titans weren't out yet. Raven floated up off the floor.

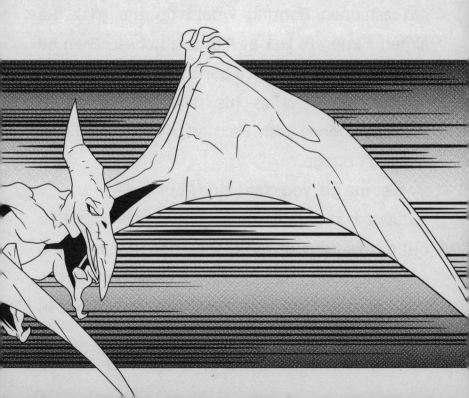

"Azarath, Metrion, Zinthos!"

As Raven chanted the words, six heavy steel canisters levitated into the air.

Whoosh! The canisters zoomed across the room, pummeling Plasmus's chest.

The blobby giant let out a mighty grunt. He pushed the canisters out of his chest. They flew back at Raven. She darted out of the way just in time.

Robin leapt from the crate. Maybe some good old-fashioned fighting would do the trick. He aimed a kung-fu kick at Plasmus's chest. Then he slammed Plasmus with a punch.

Robin cringed as his hand got stuck in Plasmus's gooey flesh. He tried to pull it out, but it wouldn't budge.

"Let me go, you giant zit!" Robin cried.

"Aaaaaaaargh!" Plasmus responded by shooting out a tidal wave of red blobby goo. Robin's hand came loose, and he sailed across the room as the goo splashed over him. Beast Boy got caught in the tidal wave, too.

"Robin!" Starfire ran to Robin's side.

Robin stood up, brushing off red ooze from his uniform. "I'm okay," he said. Then he spat out a mouthful of red goo. "Sort of."

Beast Boy stuck out his tongue. "And I thought Star's pudding tasted bad!"

Plasmus roared and pounded his chest. The Titans looked at

him wearily. Nothing they tried had worked. What should they do next?

Back in his secret headquarters, Slade watched the scene on a video screen.

"Disappointing," Slade said. "With one Titan missing, this is almost too easy. I was expecting more of a challenge."

Slade waved his hand, and Cinderblock stomped up behind him.

"Cinderblock, begin phase three," Slade ordered.

Chapter Eight

Four Against Five

Plasmus shot out another wave of red goo. This time, it covered Starfire and Raven. Starfire climbed to her feet. Red goo dripped from her long hair.

"I feel like the underside of a Zornian muck beetle," Starfire moaned.

"Tell me about it," Raven said.

Meanwhile, Plasmus had started to chase Beast Boy across the warehouse.

"Dude, I am not on the menu!" Beast Boy joked.

Plasmus closed in on Beast Boy, but Robin was right behind him. He took a grappling hook from his utility belt and hurled it.

"Maybe the best way to take you down is to tie

you up!" Robin quipped.

The hook lodged in Plasmus's blobby form. A long piece of rope was attached to the hook. Robin zipped around Plasmus, wrapping him in the rope.

The other Teen Titans joined in. Beast Boy transformed into a rhinoceros. He charged at Plasmus, knocking him on his back.

Plasmus struggled, trying to get up. But Starfire flew in, zapping him with an energy blast.

Raven finished the job by using her telekinetic powers to knock down a huge metal beam. The beam fell across Plasmus's chest, trapping him on the floor.

"We did it!" Starfire cried.

"Nice work, team!" Robin added.

Beast Boy nodded. "Yeah, didn't think we'd pull it off without —"

Raven nudged him with her elbow before he could finish. Robin didn't need to be reminded about the fight with Cyborg. Not now.

But Robin wasn't paying attention. He was checking the tiny computer on his utility belt.

"Just in time," he said. "Cinderblock's been spotted downtown."

The Teen Titans turned to leave the warehouse when they heard a noise. A squishy, oozing noise. They turned back around.

Plasmus was breaking through his bonds — by breaking himself into pieces! As the Titans watched, stunned, Plasmus separated into five pieces: one giant head and four shapeless blobs.

The Plasmus pieces grouped together and faced the Titans.

And then they charged.

The Teen Titans ran. They zoomed through two open doors into another room in the factory. Then they shut the doors behind them.

Robin pushed down a bar, locking the doors. But on the other side, Plasmus slammed all five pieces of his body against the doors. It buckled. The Titans pressed their backs against the doors, trying to keep out Plasmus.

"Four against five," Beast Boy said. "Not good odds."

Wham! Plasmus slammed against the doors again. The charge sent the metal bar flying out of place. A piece of red goo slid through the crack between the doors, nearly hitting Starfire.

Robin knew they couldn't hold the doors for long.

"Forget odds," he said. "We need a plan. Titans, separate!"

Robin, Beast Boy, Raven, and Starfire shot away

from the doors and ran farther into the room. Large, round vats of bubbling liquid filled the space. The Titans ran in different directions as the five pieces of Plasmus burst through the doors.

Starfire flew between the vats. A piece of Plasmus took the shape of a snake and sped after her. It lunged out and wrapped around her, bringing her crashing to the ground.

Beast Boy took the form of a cheetah, the swiftest animal on earth. But Plasmus was faster. One of the broken pieces took the shape of a crab and skittered after Beast Boy. A ropelike tongue shot out of the crab-blob's mouth, encircling the cheetah. Beast Boy immediately transformed into a strong gorilla, breaking the grip. But the Plasmus piece flew right back at him.

Raven found a narrow corridor of machines and flew down it. Looking behind her, she saw an octopus-shaped piece of Plasmus on her trail. Using her telekinetic powers, she caused the screws of the machines to pop out. Sharp metal pieces broke loose, slamming into Plasmus.

Raven turned around and grinned. No sign of the octo-plasmus. Her plan had worked.

Then she stopped short. Plasmus had dodged the machine parts and wriggled underneath her. Now it blocked her path, waving its tentacles.

At the same time, a piece of Plasmus was chasing Robin. It looked like a worm on legs. Robin jumped up on a wide conveyor belt to avoid it, but the creature jumped up after him.

Robin turned to face it. He steadied himself on the moving conveyor belt. Then he whipped out a long fighting stick.

"Ha! Ha!" Robin aimed blow after blow at Plasmus, trying to knock him off the track. But the wormy creature latched on to it with its sticky body and broke the stick in half.

Wham! Robin tried his best kung-fu kick, but he couldn't take down Plasmus.

All across the factory, Beast Boy, Starfire, and Raven battled the pieces of Plasmus that had attacked them. They converged in the center of the room. The head of Plasmus sat on top of a vat, watching. Beast Boy battled the red blob in his gorilla form. Starfire aimed blast after energy blast at it. Raven struggled to free herself from the grip of the blobby octopus. But they were fighting a losing battle.

Back on the conveyor belt, Robin was losing, too. The wormy piece of Plasmus had taken on the shape of a claw. It pinned Robin to the belt. The belt was moving fast — and Robin had a hunch what waited at the end.

Sure enough, as he got closer, Robin could see a vat of hot, bubbling green chemicals below him. If he didn't get free, he'd become the next ingredient in the chemical soup.

With a groan, Robin pushed up against the Plasmus piece with all his might. The claw flipped over the edge of the conveyor belt, but not before grabbing Robin by the ankle. Robin's stomach lurched as he felt himself being pulled over the side.

With lightning speed, Robin grabbed the edge of the belt with one hand. But the Plasmus claw pulled him down, and the piece he was holding on to came loose.

The metal creaked, and Robin knew it wouldn't hold much longer. Seconds later, the piece snapped off.

"Whoa!" Robin cried, as he plunged toward the vat of boiling chemicals.

Chapter Nine

Just in Time

The Plasmus piece came loose from Robin's ankle. Robin heard it sizzle as it hit the toxic soup. Robin knew he would be next.

Then, out of nowhere, a hand came down and grabbed his wrist. Robin looked up.

Cyborg grinned down at him. He hoisted Robin up onto the conveyor belt.

Cyborg powered up his right arm. "I've still got the sonic if you've got the boom," he said.

Robin nodded. He and Cyborg jumped off the conveyor belt.

In the center of the room, Plasmus had regrouped his remaining three pieces. He roared, waving his red blobby arms. The creature had

cornered Raven, Starfire, and Beast Boy.

"Teen Titans, go!" Robin and Cyborg yelled together.

The two Titans raced down the corridor toward Plasmus. They each ran up one side of the wall and flipped over, landing on the floor. Then they each flipped again, going faster. Then they flipped for the third time . . .

. . . and landed on their feet. Cyborg shot a

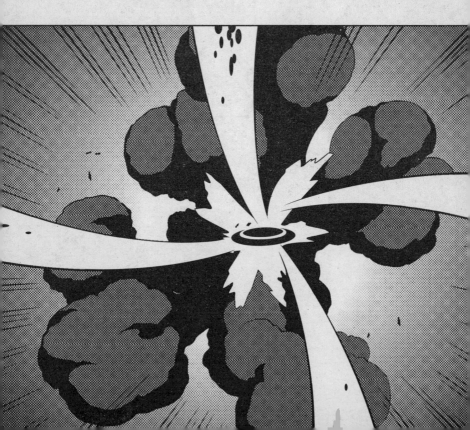

huge laser blast from his arm. At the same time, Robin released his disk. The disk exploded at the same time the laser blast reached maximum intensity.

Wham! The combined force of the attack hit Plasmus like a hurricane. Red goo splattered all over the factory.

The Sonic Boom had blasted Plasmus to bits. In his place was a thin, sleeping man — Plasmus in his human form. He lay on the floor, snoring.

Raven, Beast Boy, and Starfire struggled to their feet. Red goo dripped from their clothes and hair.

"Welcome back, Cyborg!" Beast Boy said.

Chapter Ten

Group Hug!

Seconds later, the police arrived on the scene. They had a new tank of blue liquid and quickly loaded the sleeping man inside.

Outside the factory, the Teen Titans watched as the police carted away the tank. Robin and Cyborg stood side by side, not looking at each other. Starfire, Beast Boy, and Raven waited nearby. Was Cyborg really back?

Robin shifted nervously from one foot to the other. Finally, he spoke.

"Look, uh, sorry about . . . " his voice trailed off.

"Yeah," Cyborg said, nodding.

"So, are we cool?" Robin asked.

Cyborg turned to Robin and smiled. "Frosty!"

he replied. Robin smiled back. Then he and Cyborg bumped their fists together.

Starfire jumped in the air and clapped her hands. "You made up! Glorious! I wish to initiate a group hug!"

Raven rolled her eyes.

"Yeah, yeah, yeah," Beast Boy said. "Warm fuzzies all around. But we've still got to stop Cinderblock."

"No, we don't," Cyborg said. "Thought I'd bring you a present in case you were still mad at me."

Cyborg waved his hand, and a crane pulled up. Dangling from the crane was a tall flagpole. Cinderblock was attached to the flagpole, secured tightly by bent steel beams.

"Thanks," Robin said, his eyes narrowing. "But there is one thing that's still bothering me."

Raven, Beast Boy, and Starfire gasped. Was Robin going to start another fight? They couldn't lose Cyborg again!

But that's not what Robin had in mind. "Breaking into jail? Using Plasmus to distract us? The whole plan seems too big, a little too smart for Cinderblock."

Cyborg nodded. "I've been thinking the same thing."

"Someone must have been pulling the strings," Robin said thoughtfully. The idea worried him. "But who?"

"Whoever they are, they're no match for the Teen Titans!" Cyborg said confidently.

Robin felt better. Cyborg was right. Now that
they were a team again, they could do anything.
He jumped up and gave his friend a high five.

"I heard that!" Robin cried.